# SAFARI BOUND

by Maryann Burke Deignan
and Caroline Deignan
Illustrations by Emma Duncan-Brown

A special thank you to James, Elmon, Sean and the entire team at Londolozi, a game reserve that will always be special to us.

This book is dedicated to the beautiful country of South Africa and all the people and conservation organizations who work relentlessly to protect nature and the animals that live in it.

IngramSpark
Boston, MA
maryanndeignan.com

Editing: Shayla Raquel, shaylaraquel.com
Cover Design & Illustrations: Emma Duncan-Brown, @emma.louise.illustrates
Interior Formatting: Emma Duncan-Brown

ISBN 978-1-7375960-4-2

This is a story of starry nights and lions' roars,
a place far, far away. Let your imagination soar.

It takes place in South Africa, a country
a long ways from home, in a national park
where the wild animals freely roam.

Alarm clock goes off in the early hours of dawn.
Time to get up, wake up your senses,
and stifle your yawns.

Be sure to wear sunscreen and bring
your camera, binoculars, and hat,
for the strong African sun is hard to combat.

The rangers await patiently, so climb aboard the safari jeep. Animals are stirring in the morning mist—be sure not to make a peep!

We set off on our safari, hoping for animals to be found. Keep your eyes peeled and stay focused and alert for any sounds.

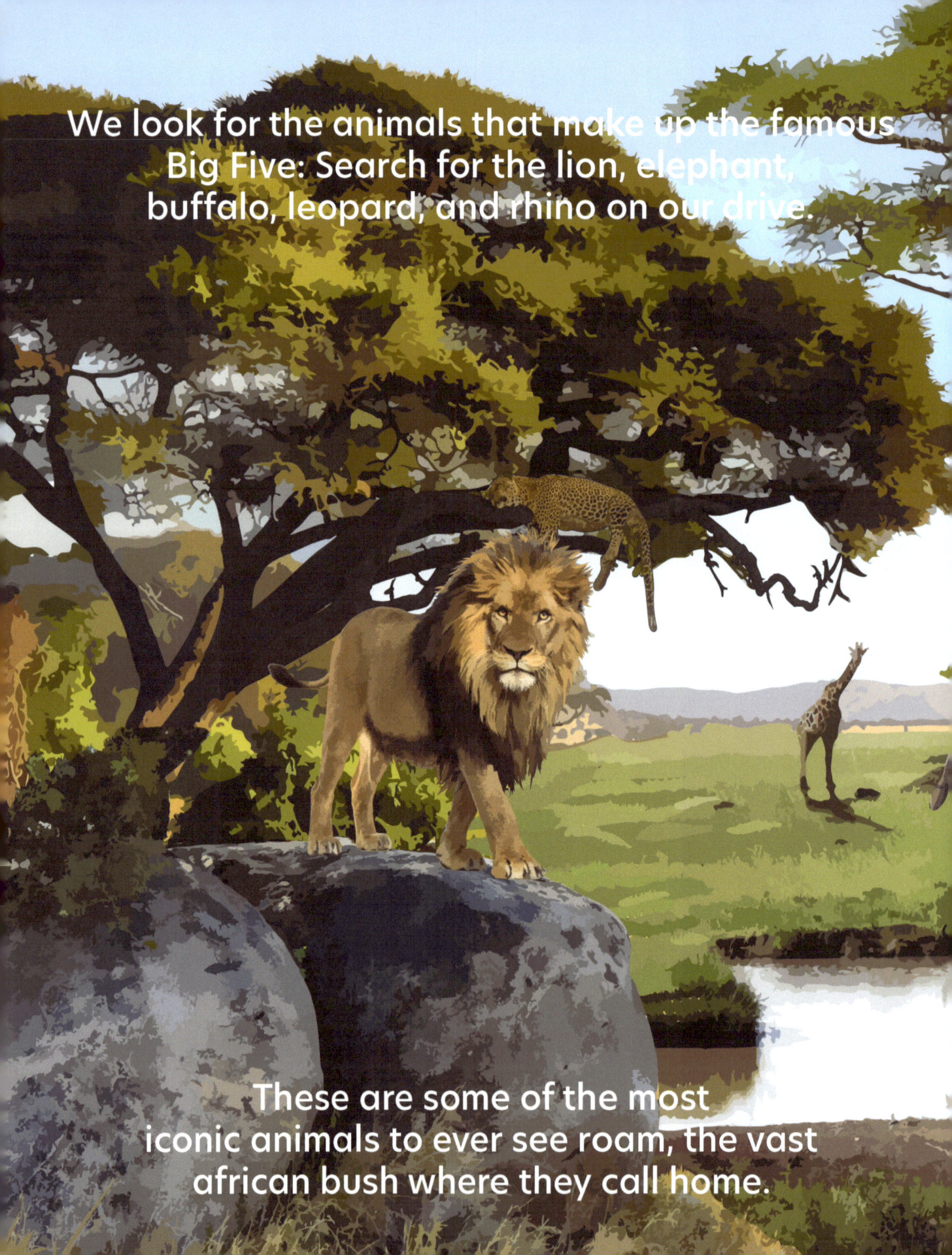

We look for the animals that make up the famous
Big Five: Search for the lion, elephant,
buffalo, leopard, and rhino on our drive.

These are some of the most
iconic animals to ever see roam, the vast
african bush where they call home.

But wait! Ears spotted! And what is that foam?
The depths of the cool water
are where the hippos call home.

Spending up to sixteen hours a day
submerged in rivers and lakes,
hippos can produce a substance similar
to sunscreen so they don't bake.

Did you know that hippos can weigh up to 12,000 pounds? But don't you worry, they can still move around! Moody in nature, expressing themselves with sneezes, grunts, and groans, these large animals like to be left alone.

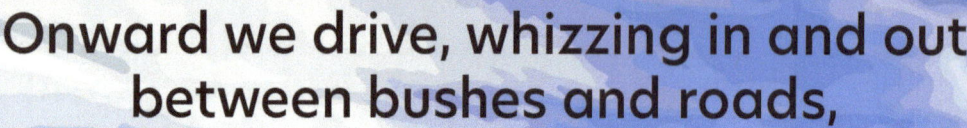

Onward we drive, whizzing in and out between bushes and roads,

keeping our eyes peeled for the tinier creatures like turtles and toads.

The Small Five hold different but important
roles in the balance of life too:
a beetle, weaver, tortoise, ant, and shrew.

The king of the kingdom is the lion, of course, who makes his presence known with mighty force.

A lion's roar can be heard from up to five miles away, a distinct warning that keeps his rivals at bay.

Throughout the lion's life, his mane
gets darker. You can be sure that he's aging,
for this sign is a marker.

Lions are the only cats that live
in groups called prides. After a big meal,
they often fall asleep on their sides.

We move on, looking for a cat
of a different type, hoping to get a glimpse
that lives up to the hype. The coat of a leopard
is unlike anything you have ever seen.

The sun bounces off their spots,
creating the most beautiful sheen.

Leopards can disguise
themselves as they slowly creep,
getting in the right position before
an unexpected leap.

Graceful and powerful, leopards
are often found high up in trees,
where they protect their food from
other animals whom they flee.

On we go, scanning for animals having
a feast. Around the next turn, a wall of gray beasts!
Did you know that white rhinos
aren't actually white?

Their name refers to their wide muzzle
that they use to bite.

Squealing and mooing, munching
on a variety of grasses,
some would say that rhinos need glasses.

The rhino's eyesight is so poor they sometimes
think trees are an enemy leering,
making the sense they rely on most, their hearing.

The largest of the land animals
awaits us at the bend.
Elephants are a female-led species
and an intelligent friend.

Staying together in groups
called herds, their big, powerful backs
are often perched with birds.

Elephants are playful and able
to express feelings like you or me,
even swishing their tails side
to side when they feel glee.

They trumpet into the morning with
raised trunks before they charge into
the cool water for a midmorning dunk.

We turn our heads, and what do we see?
The neck of a giraffe poking through a tree.

Giraffes are the tallest living animal on earth.
Their babies are able to stand within thirty minutes
of birth!

Giraffes are giants who are sneaky thieves of Mother Nature's acacia trees and leaves.

Usually quiet, with the occasional hum, snort, groan, and grunt, giraffes have an intricate design of star-shaped spots down their front.

As we drive back to camp, we see
the black-and-white glint of a dazzle of zebras
breaking out into a sprint.

The zebras' stripes are important to keep
them safe and cool,
but look carefully, for their stripes can fool!

When zebras group and put their coats together to mix, it is their predators that they can trick.

As we hear the high-pitched bark of the zebras when they bray, our smiles widen and we head back to camp to call it a day.

Now that you've been introduced to Africa's animals and landscape, use your imagination to see which animal takes shape.

Are you the lion, leopard, hippo, or ant?
Call out your choice—roar, grunt, snort, or pant!

Sit still and listen really well.
Tap into your animal instincts, even use your smell.

The time has come to see if YOU can hear
the distant animal noises in your ear.

The adventure ahead
is yours for the taking, the details
are your imaginations making.

Get ready, get excited,
maybe even jump around.
You're about to be
**SAFARI BOUND!**

## About the author: Maryann B. Deignan

Maryann is a retired teacher and childcare director with over forty years of teaching children of all ages and abilities. Maryann and Caroline were inspired to write Safari Bound after a special experience visiting South Africa. Maryann now resides in Charlestown with her husband of 35 years, Chris. She hopes that Safari Bound will ignite a spark in the imaginations of children everywhere.

## About the author: Caroline Deignan

Caroline, Maryann's daughter, has also loved working with and caring for children over the last twelve years. She currently works in the public health space in South Africa where she has lived for the last six years. Caroline is an outdoors enthusiast who enjoys hiking, swimming, running, and yoga. Safari Bound is Caroline's first children's book.

www.ingramcontent.com/pod-product-compliance
Lightning Source LLC
Chambersburg PA
CBHW041006170626
46815CB00002B/191

* 9 7 8 1 7 3 7 5 9 6 0 4 2 *